Roses & Thorns

A
Collection Of Poems

Roses & Thorns

Obiorah Momife

Lampstand Books
Lagos, Nigeria.

obimomife@yahoo.com

Roses and Thorns
A Collection of Poems

ISBN: 978-978-915-747-1

Published By Lampstand Books
9, Ayotola Close, Off Isasi,
Akute via Ojodu, Lagos, Nigeria.
Tel: +234 1 4345740, +234 802 334 9033,
Email: lampstand@yahoo.com

This book is Dedicated to

Mrs. Edith Ofili-Okonkwo, and all who labour in love every day, everywhere, to uphold the divine covenant of marriage...

Acknowledgements

To God Almighty who allowed the challenges that inspired this book, who grants me great grace to still be on this side of life with hope alive.

To Henry Ogufere, I owe a debt I can never ever repay.

Austyn Njoku, Dotun Saseyi, Ogochukwu Nweke, Igeme Ezenwata, Mohammed Dodo, Peter Ogudoro, Odiobara Aizek, for pruning and oiling the feathers of this book to soar unrestrained… many thanks.

To, Uri Ukoha Kalu, Ngozi Mbonuike, Olisemeka Obi, Chijioke Odeluga,
Gordy Oshoko, James Odubena, Biodun Taiwo, Chuka &Nk Onwuamaegbu; your little drops has become a flowing river.

Timothy Fakrogha, Funminiyi Odetayo, Jide Odutayo, Ikechukwu Amadike, Nnamdi Duru, Chidebem Oba, Imemba Obi, Funmi Akomolafe, Alice Odum, Tunde Alao, Tunde Ayeni, Nkechi Maduekwe, Paul Moses, Ese Bob-Okonedo, Doris Azeke, Kenechukwu Onyenorah, Nicole Ezomo, Agatha Umurieho, Chris Uchegbu, Talib Kolo, Fabian Ndubuisi, Nkechi Ntia-James, Blessing Afekhai, and others too many to mention here, in my heart you remain invaluable.

To my team mates, Sumitra Vilairasd, Bunmi Ebhomenye, Foluso Makanjuola, Jane Patrick- Onuh, Isabelle Lasserre, and Kalu Ume; your support is priceless.

To Apostle Anselm Madubuko, your meekness gives me so much strength.

Pastor and Mrs. Don Lawrence and the members of Life Builders House, Ogba, Lagos State, Nigeria, I appreciate your care.

And to my family and 'true friends', who continue to give godly counsel… your life will be filled with more of roses than thorns.

LOVE

Love is like ice
Sometimes it's cold
Love is like spice
Sometimes become hot
Love is like honey
Sometimes very sweet
Love is like wormwood
At times become bitter
Love is like rose flower
It has roses and thorns
Love is like a pond
Sometimes so stagnant
Love is like a tree
Swings with the wind
Love is like the sun
Brightens broken souls
Love is like the moon
A balm for darkness
Love is like the rain
Bringing hope to all
Love is like the dews
Makes the heart float
Love is a gift encased
Unwrapped by sharing…

11th March, 2011.

COLOUR OF LOVE

Somewhere in our heart
Between the deep valleys
Of grief and happiness
Of falsehood and reality
Of roses and sharp spikes
Of cruelty and sympathy
Of poverty and prosperity
Of hostility and harmony
Of darkness and brightness
Of predators and their preys
Openly stands bridges…

Somewhere in our heart
Like the colourful rainbow
That comes after a feral rain
This bridge stands to restore
The hope torn from our reach
By the madness in our cities

With the cement of patience
This bridge will be erected
With the steel of meekness
Its foundation will be set up
By the certain colour of love
It will eternally be sustained.

6th April, 2003.

THIS LOVE

This love is like the clouds
So heavy with rain
But they cannot drop
This love is like the sun
Desires to brighten everywhere
But subdued by fogs of offense
This love is like the breeze
Gentle and soothing
Yet unable to blow air
This love is like the sea
With a so many treasures
So feeble can't flow downhill
This love is like the earth
Her bowels yearning for seed
But like a clam it is sealed
This love is like roses
With butterflies and bees attending
But her petals are locked up today

25th Feb., 2011.

FAILING IN LOVE

She locks her heart
The keys lost in the sea
Where no hand can reach
Where her hand can't reach
So as not to change her mind
And return again to love

On my knees for years, I plead
For her heart, her love
Even one-tenth…

Willing to give her
All of my heart so tender
Like fresh buds of rose flower
She took it
She crushed it
Like orphaned cereals
In the grating hands
Of some drugged millstone…

While I struggle in the currents
Of hot tears shed for love
She smiles waving goodbye
Reclining in another pleasure boat ….

SCARS ON MY FLESH

I have seen love
I have also seen wickedness
Indifference from the one I love
Hurts me the most

I have seen laughter
I have seen pain
But misery of the one I chose
Humbles me the most

I have heard glad tidings
I have heard awful rumours
But arrows from my brother's bow
Strikes me the hardest…

I have seen light
Have also seen darkness
But the colours of this rose
And its scent makes me forget
The thorns and scars on my flesh
The thorns and the scars from a rose …!

22nd Aug., 2009.

INATTENTION

I wish I could sing songs
In harmonious tunes
With the voice of angels
To assemble by my side
Millions of keen admirers

I wish I can write songs
With great lively rhymes
Songs that live forever
Rhymes that flow together
As roses and thorns closer

I would sing my song
I would strike the chords
Of my desolate guitar
To rhyme with my heartbeat
To resound the loneliness
Of a life seeking affection

But I can sing!
I can play my music
I can be my own critic
I can be my own friend
Yes, I will sing my song
In the opera of my soul
And enjoy my gloomy life
Riding the arc of the rainbow…

12th September, 2002.

NEW SONG

I am waiting for
A song of liberation
Never heard in this land
Where songs flow freely as waterfalls

I am searching
The sky for freedom
From our heaving holes
But despair looms in the horizon

I see everyone grope
In the dark for a smile
Quadruped, bare on the floor
For a song that seems extinct

Like hordes of termites
Lost in an old labyrinth
I see them flee from fire of thorns
Auctioning their wares as men under spell
Going to dwell in the cold…

But who will take up the mantle
As a father, begin to lead
As a man, begin to love
As a priest, begin to pray…

21st Aug. 2003.

OLIVE

I saw a plant elevated high
Like a banner raised for peace
I stretched my hands to reach it
And it was so silky in my hands

Will he tell her he got a seed?
Will she believe it is a revelation?
Let her receive it as a vision also
So they will both work things out

In our hands are times and seasons
But this is the time for the olive tree
To grow into beautiful budding twigs
Even among our hard stones and sands

UNTOUCHABLE

She is like a red rose
Beautiful, but unfriendly
Roses delight butterflies
Bees skip at their sweetness
Hummingbirds too, at their luster
Yet they remain roses showing their glow
Not recoiling even from bovines in the field
And they are the most beautiful in the world…

Her skin is lively and silky
Can only see and smell her from afar
And like touch-me-not you cannot feel her
She shuts down her leaves from any embrace
As the mimosa her love shies away from fondness
As a termite will become a feast for the patient frog.

11th Aug., 2010.

CLOSED GATES

Where cometh this pain
That dries up every source
Leaving everyone in disdain

Where cometh this bitterness
Angels becoming so insensitive
Desiccating all their sweetness

Where cometh this resentment
Silky petals becoming baked barbs
Unaware it's a trip to confinement

Where cometh these battle cries
The burgle calls and drawn daggers
In field and new tunnels in our cities

Where cometh these backsliders
Permitting fables to level their gate
And leaving their walls to plunderers

Someday this gate will be unlocked
Open to the brightness of forgiveness
And all critical voices forever silenced.

29th March, 2011.

ALABASTER OIL

She is a delight to observe
Her charm simply appealing
Her life is goodly and unassuming
Her words peaceful like clear waters
Her shadow a guide from obscurity

And I am drawn to her…

Everyone loves and says good of her
Saw her in a fight once against injustice
Saw her so enraged once as her spouse
Writhe in pain

I know she is drawn to me…

Her young line up like ducklings
As she leads them daily to the brooks
And she stands as a mirror to them…

She dwells daily in her Lord's court
Pouring her alabaster oil at his feet
With her glory washing his shame
And she is growing without thorns
Blooming like a rose from beyond

Like fireflies her glow pulls me to her…

14th Nov., 2009.

SACRIFICE

A lovely garden set by the Almighty
With pure priceless seeds to bloom
And gave them to prune and guard
But they turn the turf to a war zone
Exposing, tearing down their cover
Endorsing an access for the accuser

Now with him is their seal of harmony
Ten thousand that need to be in flight
Are all quadrupeds, roaming in the fields
And they cope with a scanty thousand

Wild spikes grow choking the roses
As they blindly romance this plague
Naïve; they are malignant like cancer
And as magma will flow to their seed
And turn everything into a wasteland

The Father in heaven awaits the day
They will come to the understanding
The mystery of transforming to babes
Humbly considering the other better

Yes, the Lord is waiting for that day
When unity of the trinity manifesting
Unfurls like a flower in our families
And with the barrier of self shattered
True tranquility will come attending…

11th July, 2009.

TILL THE END

They took off so well like diamonds
Forever to shine, then he stumbled…

She has done so well holding forth
But she was sent for a time like this
To help bring him again to his feet
So his heart will trust in her forever…

In anxiety he grumbles and fumbles
May never get back without a pat…

Slowly her heart drudges down daily
A guiltless weight carried ignorantly
And he has now become a castaway
For being unable to track their lead

But is he not the one to show the way
And she to follow though as equals?

His counsel is like water on a rock
Like warmth on a blazing charcoal
His commendations are distasteful
Like the bad breath of an adversary

One is to put to flight a thousand
Two in accord get additional spoils
In disagreement they spoil everything

Their vow was for better or worse
To stay as one and mould godly seeds
Passing virtues to the next generation

As they submit one to another in love

Her reward will be golden like Sarah's
Following, even lying to keep her man
But she must continue till the very end
Not like Lot's salty mate backwards look.

6th July, 2009.

FREEZING POINT

Everything begins to get cold
Garments of praise turning old
Altars of prayer festers mould
Hands of love start to withhold
Souls saved strays from bound
And all begin to scratch for gold
Unmindful where they are found…

Their head swells with new horns
In their heart a wild inferno burns
Like a new kiln they rage to ashes
Their limb like lost wind flies fast
All they ever seek does not persist
The sweet roses they adore die first
Thorns detested turns test for a rest…

8th March, 2011.

COLD MILDEW

Some stronger than you are broke
Some holier than you are cast off
    Some more connected are lost
Some more beautiful are single
Some more gifted are unknown…

Why does she think she is perfect?
Her crest stuck-up like a peacock
Her ears caustic to every reproof
Warnings drop on her stony heart
Like water tumbling off a dry rock

She hounds all but her puppeteer
His fire burns and burns and dies out
For there is no more wood in the house
His love burns and burns and dies out
As he screams in the woods voiceless

2nd Aug., 2009.

BATTLEFIELD

From afar this flower looks velvety
Everyone speaks of its smoothness
But at her home her love is atrocious
Like a cactus, thorns litter her body

What ails her no one seems to know
And she is filled with endless anguish
Yet in the sanctuary she dances daily
Lifting her hands so high in ecstasy
While her mate is trapped in a maze

The ones who adore her she detests
The ones who exploit her she adores...

She has an oath before this covenant
And plans to fulfill it despite the odds
A scheme that must be accomplished
By eerie hands lurking in the shadows

They live as those who are haunted
As their blades devour day by day
Ignorant their evil seed of bitterness
Could linger unto many generations

As they begin to rigmarole in the city
Traversing the valleys and dry brooks
Only getting to the edge of liberation
From the heaviness of familial fiends

For his love his wings are trimmed
For his timidity his ears are blocked

For his virtue this wilderness swells
And for his destiny this battle rages

28th July, 2009

DRY WELLS

He is supposed to drink from his well
But it is stuffed and he dies of thirst
He is not to drink from another well
For it is death to his seed
But to the owner it is life

Where have the gatekeepers gone to
Who are not double-tongued for gain?
Themselves drink not from other's well
But with their blood stand on the truth
A battered casualty in the raging war
Declared long ago in Eden's Garden…

Should a well not yield her water freely?
And not defraud her cover its sweetness…

What rose will with pride deny herself
The timely visitations of the busy bees
Her pollen is only honey when released
Held back it becomes only sweet spleen
Like waters in a pond grimy and bitter!

29th July, 2009.

REALITIES

As they walked the aisles it was bliss
But these days they cannot even kiss
And now their lives know no peace
As they sail blindly in the misty seas

She says; do your own, I'll do mine
So that everyone would be all right
She desires to be the only sunlight
But her shine is a chime of grime

His hands are too small to cuddle her
His legs are too short to walk with her
His eyes are dim they can't trace her
Does any link still hold them together?

They hear always that life is too short
Yet heed Satan's whispers and report
Letting resentment their destiny abort
Throwing down the gate to his cohort

Like an old toy his place is in a box
A rose plant scheming its growing rose
An old gramophone now without a voice
Is there warmth in a flea- bitten fleece?

July, 2009.

GATE CRASHERS

Her hands soulfully travel down
Into the starved depth of my bosom
As the root of the upside-down tree
Searching for fluid in a wasteland

Her embrace so soft like a new fur
Bringing back memories of yesterday
When our path was lined with thrills
Our cradle with brilliant rose flowers

She starts sowing kisses on my cheek
Holding so tightly to me like a leach
That just found a plump bloody vein

Together our tears begin to swell
The rains pouring too in torrents
Yet the ground remains parched
As our early seed refuses to sprout

Looking up to discern her identity
Alas! A façade of a fiendish fantasy
One I parted ways with in the past
Crashing in through my naive mind

She has found me out once again
Pulling down walls all around me
While my watchman stays dozing!

24th April, 2006.

LOLLIPOP

For a displeasure not apparent
She shuts the gate to her holy city
The healing balm that tranquillizes
Willfully opening a gap for the thief…

And daily he sorts for lasting peace
But her hot balloon begins to boil
Unable to land on his bed of thorns

He asks, "Did I not pray well?
Is this not the bone of my bones?"
And millions bomb heaven daily
Seeking for a moment of this life…

Keep the grass from the goat
It will delight in thy neighbours'
Keep thy holy city from thy priest
Might begin to minister to strangers

Some take pleasure in the lollipop
They eat the sweet and burn the stick
They get the roses and burn the thorns

Hastily she seeks to go her way
Third one in the covenant she ignores
The one the oath was taken at his feet
She claims to have a covenant with Him
Raising holy hands before him in prayers

5th July, 2009.

RAIN MAKER

The rose in my garden stays its smell
Because I cannot make rains anymore
But dews from above swell her vessel
Yet she keeps her perfume far from me

This rose with thorns in my backyard
Wants to become the lone rain maker
So all will know my cloud is empty
And my whirlwind now a mild breeze

Can she be a rose and a rainmaker
Sun to travel round calling up waters
The wind flying about scattering rain
And a eunuch defying lilies in streams?

This lovely fertile rose in my garden
Reclines daily from my tender touch
Declines the desire to brighten us up
Yet outside becomes nectar for bees…

27th Aug., 2009.

COLOUR BLIND

Pretty women are like roses flowers
Pluck them home they begin to fade
They will tell everyone they love you
They will never say to you, "I love you"
Like a robot they'll wish to control you
They will tell everybody you are so lazy
And they'll begin to think you are crazy
For loving a woman who loves another
She screams she is regarded unfaithful
Yet air she breathes how meaningful?
Allowing all those leeches to hang on
Bleeding and milking her and having fun
And these are those who appreciate her…

Lines of fading tunes of adoration
Still linger in my wrecked ego
But before me these gaping gates
O! What choices to be made
Heard that faith needs patience
So as to receive the promise
So what choices of brightness
Preludes these thorns of dimness…

This cross I must bear to the end
Maybe my pride its pain will mend

2nd Sept., 2009.

SHADOWS

She's become so free like a bird
Released from a very old prison
She goes out whenever she likes
Comes back odd times she thinks
Like a stray sheep she's satisfied
She puts on whatever she desires
Whether as a village masquerade
Or as all these urban society girlies
With their sensational make-ups
Her worshippers openly applaud.

Naïve and with so many troubles
Tons of thorns pile on his head
Will his rose bloom in a new garden?
Will it be but a season for the rains?
To unearth all the shadows lurking
Trying to freeze a destiny raw as gold…

3rd Sept., 2009.

THE MONGER

There is no mirror in her house
She peeps into other people's own
Then her tongue flies like a sparrow…

She is a seasoned spinster
But will her hand be asked for?

I hear she prays and waits
For a brother in a distant land
Please tell him to come take her away!

Her leaves are fading
Her thorns now so bare
And no one can tell her
Yet her seers say she shines…

She is a spider
Tears down homes
To build her own house
Yet she does not have a mirror…

5th Sept., 2009.

THURAYA

There goes the mask that shields her
The veil that shields her depravity
A circlet she sorts diligently…

Here comes that primordial monster
On a pale pony with a hard harness
In her hands mutant roses with spiky edges
Flying about as whirlwinds
In her tongue-twisted tales of thorns piercing

As the crown buckles to the roost
She ascends the heights to dominate
A people sightless with naked eyes
They drink delightfully from dirty pools
Yet they sit upon uncommon treasures!

6th Sept., 2009.

DISENGAGEMENT

She seized the fruits from his branch
Secretly shielding as battering ram
Crassly crushing them in her anguish
Tender daffodils in morning bloom
Seeds sown in tears in good grounds…

Like fresh feathers she is tossed
By winds of her primitive coveting
The disorder of her childlike musing
Cannot see this bend is not an end

But like the profligate son's father
I will wait patiently for her return
Though I stomach this testing thorn
Maybe she will come back healthier
Unless the Lord wills this disconnect

6th Sept., 2009.

BOTTOM-LINE

He tries to join the train on a ride
But the gate is shut from the inside
And the keys thrown away outside
The lamb sits on the lion for a ride

It was a pleasing passage of roses
The blues, the reds and the whites
On the line also were the prickles
And now the wave of wrinkles

If they wait till the end to be saved
What if one drops before the bend…

Better to be devoured in the street
By ashless firewood in severe heat
Than at home in a degenerate pit

This battle is set as a mind journey
As plain paths become very thorny
As bland buds are spread with honey
The bottom-line is all about money

08th Sept., 2009.

NINE NINE NINE

Rose early upon a mount to travail
At descent she was there on my tail
As she trucked the world for a spoil
Was it warmth that has gone stale?
A concealed loathing rediscovered
Or a heart so hard it can never fail

And the month was tagged freedom

Three men in black with their arms
Paid to support the pain she brings
The cut so exact and deeply bleeds
They said, "Pastor, give us water!"
The retribution they seek to deter

Hurray! It is a month of freedom…

Came with an automated broom
Openly shaming her dated groom
Was this plan set from the prime?
Or she dances to a galling rhyme
Predestined from unknown groves…

And she drove away with her freedom…

9th Sept., 2009.

PATIENCE

A sneering smile on her face
She schemed for me to drown
She is transformed from light
Into despair of deep darkness
Of grueling grills without guilt…!

In her hands my tender olives…

I took another look and saw
Standing close was the Lord
In this cascade of tough tears
Restraining me from my sword
This battle is mine and not yours…

His lovely hands stretched out
Saying, "Hold unto my hands,
I am here to preserve your soul
This rose comes with proud thorns
That only divine fire can overcome…"

You will be with your olive branches

29th Sept. 2009.

LIVING WATERS

Did she stray away?
Did she go astray…?

He waits for her to come back
To continue the devoted task
Deserted because of a crack…

But she has to be transformed
Unseen ominous cloak placed
On her childish collars cracked…

Her ears deafened to ire of serpents
Ceases to make friendly foes friends
And a life thrilling everybody ends…

I hear a voice say, "This shall pass
These prickly thorns will be burnt
And new rose flowers will sprout
As fresh spring of living water flow"

18th Oct., 2009.

WILD ROSE

Stands out in the garden
Countless beautiful petals
Like lilies brighten the valleys
All celebrate her late crowning

Like a sow in a sty she is fat
In her fatness she is depraved
In her lewdness she sings praises
As all praise and call her blessed

She sees a brute that is so lost
Her doubt for the future swells
With her are her seer and priest
That sees a tool without a voice
But with them a lonely wise man
That prays his wings to grow again

She is now spiky like wild roses
With a bizarre exotic fragrance
The winds stand for her butterfly
Sweet counsel becomes bitter pills
As she cruises even without a sigh

22nd Oct., 2009.

PURIFICATION

Held back the tears from falling
Like the clouds they swell inside
Trying to rip the banks of my soul
They say a man should not whine
So he wouldn't be tagged a woman
He should not be soft like the roses
But tough and thorny to be feared
I do not intend to restrain these tears
From falling on these parched grounds
And burst in countless smithereens…

I will take this shame and freely cry
Like the skies to unburden my weight
I'll shed these tears in selfless torrents
Purifying my mind, my heart and soul…

24th Oct., 2009.

CONSCIENCE

She said, “I won’t love again”
Warnings about him are true
To ruin my dream and destiny
I was blinded because of love
And for years remained a fool

Into this emptiness and anguish
The past seems better than today
Tomorrow pictures a mere mirage…

Would not believe you anymore
Continue to beat your dead drums
I won’t listen to its morbid rhythm
Drag down the roof over my head
For the rains to pour down freely
It will become open heaven for me
Like the time you seized my wings
And I discovered who my source is…

Would no longer listen to your lies
That life comes without any thorns
Leading me to dark paths of doubt
Gloom soiled with musk of anguish
In the besieged heart of your victims
Veiled from the Lord’s faithfulness!

5th Aug., 2009.

TIME

No matter if the roses in my garden fade
No matter if the pain in my heart stays
No matter if these false accusations persist
No matter if this flood continues on my head
No matter if the wall of this vale gets slimy
No matter if nobody appears for my rescue
No matter if these old thorns and thistles live
No matter if the sun refuses to rise again…

I have determined to wait for you
To travail until the gloomy cloak falls
To ignore strange voices from the city
I am sure you will come back reformed
Then I would be strong and transformed
For the Lord decreed it from His holy hills
And upon His word I am going to stand…

2nd Nov., 2009.

COLDNESS

Burdened by hope in potent paddocks
Left behind by love to expire at twilight
Her heart blistering on a new barbecue
As he languishes, freeing a distended one

Like a balloon taking a tour amid spikes
Like a mole trying the tides with reptiles
Before everyone lies his hope in shreds

And now she is mislaid in mire to grope
To grope for warmth from a cuddle lost
A hold gone to the gale of yesteryears
To the boisterous wind of cold intimacy

Glittering garden sowed for their pruning
Assembles sleepy spikes and tired thorns
Yet they continue in the iron-barred cage
He strangles her with pale blameless roses
She smokes him with her untamed thorns

Even if your eyes are like the clear skies
Shadows will always remain in their heart
So you will never see those sinister splits
And what invites their sightless minions

And there is going to be the cold nights…

3rd April, 2010.

RE-BIRTH

That affection is too cold like ice
Her tongues twirls twisted in lies
Like the night her embrace is still
As the moon descending downhill

This love is stuffy from filthiness
Of foul fingers of false friendship
Foes clutching as leeches for juice
And they appear with sugary sting

The cloud they raise is fully empty
They will never bring down the dews
The dusts they carry seem so heavy
But they only come as sweet breeze

I will smile again with the sunflower
On the pathway that mirrors sunlight
I will sing again in the running shower
As this fogginess flees for my daylight

03rd Aug., 2010.

UNBROKEN

They will quote all the scriptures
From Genesis down to Revelation
They will speak in diverse tongues
That even angels become so green
And they walk like one so spiritual
But they are completely unbroken
Their hearts clutching to the world

They'll train the nightingale to sing
Moon and the sun stoop for them
When they travail the walls quake
Yet they remain totally unbroken
Secretly holding to material gain

To every cause they drop a cheque
Every tongue resounds their praise
But they are not yet broken within
For their soul is not given to God

Like a time-bomb they are waiting
For the time to implode or explode
Like the proverbial Wall of Siloam
Countless will come crashing down
In these terrible thermal thumps!

If blindly you find a beautiful rose
Whose heart is deeply in the world
Without discovering thorns within
If you live it will be with memories
A bitter thirst and a deep cut…

MARIONETTE

Who is that string-puppet?
Who is the puppeteer…?

She is made to be the heart
To function as one together
But in folly they strive for filth
When they ought to wait in bliss
God's preferred and peculiar…

Show me a heart without a head
Show me a head without a heart
Show me roses devoid of thorns
Even puppies know better to play
As one falls for the other, and they
Both go their way wagging happily…

28th March, 2009.

APOCALYPSE

What will happen if they shatter
The bridge that links them together
If one of them goes upstream, the other
Flows with the cruel currents downhill?

What will happen if darkness that lurks
In the hearts of these stray sheep, drops
And the inferno in their route rekindles
Revealing the scrap shielding their eyes?

What will happen when their eyes open
And all they call friends turn out as foes
And those locked out become true allies
That for years plead for their restoration?

What will happen if these hearts of stone
Are transformed into fresh hearts of flesh?
What will happen if the pain they suffer
Turns to joy and is allowed in as a guest?

What will happen if the Master's statute
For the one to love and the other to submit
Is considered wholly without philosophies
Wouldn't our homes become paradises?

16th March, 2009.

DELUSION

They tried to untie the knot -
They went opposite ways
Yes they did…
But did they truly unknot the ties…

It is unforgiveness
And the hardness that sit deep
In their unregenerate hearts
That has done this…

The wish to go their own ways
With water from a broken gourd
With seed that does not exist
If they never tied the nuptial knot
They recoil from experience
A memory that will bring regrets

And they boast of what they brought
Into the ship they could not salvage
From the boisterous hands of the sea
They jettison all they have laboured for
And a future they could not wait for
Couldn't see mirage is only a mile away
A mirage that beckons them to illusion…

7th April, 2010.

SCARLET

The traffic is on a fast track
So many are dying to enter
Some are fleeing with scars
Marks from their self vanity…
Some dare the hills for seers
To disclose each false player
Others travel to deep valleys
For a sign of whom and when
Some will not even dare go in
Or feel it with a stretched shaft
For fright of prickles than roses
Yet it is a natural act from God
To resound the harmony above
Among His people on the earth

23rd March 2009.

TWO INTO ONE

I still remember this couple
Lived in my neighbourhood
Every day they barter blows
While they scream and curse
And every one would assemble
Soon you see them hugging
Cuddling, as unruffled lovers
As if nothing ever took place…

They just didn't care about us

Used to think they were crazy…
But were they really insane?

Considered him so obstinate
Like an aged grumpy donkey
Also thought her to be wild
Like a steed none would dare

They will laugh so doubtfully
They did not care if we stared
Sour gossip flows freely from
Every tongue, young and old

Yet, they just lived their lives…

Never saw them bring folks in
Or friendly foes as counselors
They continued trying, failing
Falling, growing, and winning…

Soon we all began to wonder
Why our morning rooster failed
Why our dissonant lullabies faded…

5th April, 2009.

UPS AND DOWNS

Without pain on earth
Who would understand joy?

Without the failings of man
Would amnesty make sense?

Without feelings of solitude
Who would value relationships?

Without thorns in paths of life
Who would struggle for glory?

Without an experience of burden
Would freedom have any meaning?

Without the spasms of starvation
Who would relish unsavoury meals?

Without valleys and the mountains
Won't the earth's plains be boring?

Without the evil called man's heart
Kindness would never become virtue!

Without the dilemma called a woman
Is there a better puppet called man?

4th August, 2009.

CLEOPATRA

Sits on her tavern of luxury
Guzzling the wine of iniquity…

She lives in barred districts
Swims in the brook of doom
Floats in the cloud of misery
Feasts in the bloody shrines
Of sorcerers and charlatans
She travels at soaring speed
On the highway of murkiness
Does not care for tomorrow…

By morning they fade away
As vapour before the sun
Petals of true sweet roses
Turned into cruel foliages
Accursed from conception
Thorns of pain for eternity
Lost not to be seen again
On the way of brightness
Pathway of perseverance
The true way to the promise…

7th November, 2003.

PEACOCK DANCE

She does not know intimacy
Cannot contain others view
Yet cries her heart out for love

She knows not forgiveness
So many are in her offence list
Yet moans why she is not liked

She knows not true friendship
A tool used for so many seasons
Yet worries why no one cares

Her ears are used to a melody
Songs of tribute and adulation
She knows no note of censure

She sits in the shadowy vanity
Knows not of its dim grimy pit
As a mule she is tied to this yoke
Yet does not know help is within

Like balloons she wants to escape
But can't stand fiery flames or heat
Like a rose she wants to blossom
But must learn to cohabit with spikes…

10th May, 2008.

PRICKLED ROSES

Breathlessly he drank the milk
Flowing from her sacred rivulet
A trip to the city of red roses…

She served him in a teaspoon
The milk of her foggy fantasy
On a moonless gloomy night
Unwilling yet with a chuckle…

She shrunk into her cocoon
Clothed with festering pride
A highway to misfortune…

His ego goes now for a ride
For this splintered omnibus…

26th January,.2004.

LINE SQUALL

Walls divide as their hearts unite
For few minutes birds stop singing
Every creation in hush falls asleep…

Suddenly he screams "I am locked
In a hug with a deadly python and it is
Squeezing the spirit out of me…!"

Should I weep without tears
Behind the curtain of shame?
Should I keep quiet for fame?

Behind the veil of frustration
Should I scream without shame?
As one coupled in a frosty flame

Should I sheepishly smile in awe
Behind ancient thicket of thorns
Lost in time with crooked crowds?

As the prize of roses melt away
And my feeble fingers are battered
By barbed blades of barrenness…!

Is this a trip without a compass
Or a voyage without a destination?
Alas the strong horses fade away!

21st April, 2009.

LIFE IS LIFE

The offspring of a snake
Will be a snake
If the father is a snake
The more of a snake it will be…

Have you seen a snake without a snake as a father?
Or a snake whose mother is not a snake
A snake might withhold its sting
Does it make it a lizard?
A snake is a snake with or without a sting!

Like a man is a man
Whether he dangles like a pendulum or not
A man cannot be a woman
Because he puts on a wig
Or wears a lipstick
He is a man because he is a man
That a man falls does he become a woman?
Still, he needs a woman to rise sometimes…

A woman is a woman
Whether she is rich and beautiful
Or if she is poor and dreadful
She is still a woman
That she nags and fights does not make her a man
There is still a way to her tender heart
She is a woman because she is a woman
And will always remain a woman…

A rose flower is a rose flower
Whether it be white, red, pink or yellow

A rose is a rose
A rose is not a rose without its thorns
A rose flower and its thorns make a rose…

Life is life uphill or down the vale
In the ghetto or in the metropolis
The power, pleasures, and pain of life
    A discovery that comes afterwards!
So as a snake, a man, or a woman,
Or as a rose flower
Life is life

20th May, 2009.

THE PAIN

It hurts, still suffer it now
When I see her, it comes back
The force for reprisal pulling
But I am constrained by love

One says that I am deluded…!

Everywhere I turn
I hear fables so conjured
Plots crafted with tapestries
Of vileness and naivety
All doors close against me
As they all cannot discern
That I am not so bestial
To ignite my own bosom

She must be broken or she'll kill you…!

Like a rose, try to break her
Then you completely crush her

Got to forgive and let God
Heal me of this hurt that I bear
I'm going to come out victorious
Flying high without any weight…

August, 2009.

IN LIMBO

A garden grows in their courtyard
The petals radiate from a distance
Like those of a bright crimson rose
Butterflies visit at day, bats at night…

Suck her nectar and you will expire
Pluck her flowers and, starved spikes
Waiting to drain any blameless blood
Like greedy talons will swoop on you

She is glad everyone as hungry bees
Floats around her disappearing glow
And not able to perch for warmness
Except for those altered to androids

Will the dawn of the wrinkles abate?
What the silkiness of youth repelled
Will the strange yearning for revenge
Bring calm chaste seeds need to grow

Will this infighting heal the dryness?
Plaguing a land and people ignorant
A price is placed to exterminate them
For not extending the seed of infidelity

And blindly he clings to these leeches…!
Unaware they only live a borrowed life

21st April, 2009.

SIREN

She flogs her daughter naked in the open
Then weeps when she is raped tomorrow

She tells everyone that his crown is weak
Then wonder why they bow not to her

'He is thorns', blares the siren everywhere
Unworthy strangers counseling so sweetly
He deserves to be respected and honoured

She as sweet roses needs a lid from the sun
Slumbers at her mother's manipulating laps
Like one whose mind is preset for eruption
Yet sobs and moans as one in a cuddly crib

On the dais he stands to preach everyday…
With audience as pebbles and mute gravels

Who plucked the roses in their brilliance?
Should a lone rose smell as a rose garden?

13th April, 2009.

NUPTIAL FLIGHT

Finally, the carnival ends…

They say she is indulged
Indolent and cannot cook
Knows nothing about respect
Every day and every night
Like a fresh turbine she nags
Everything must be done her way
And all must see through her eyes
Men are switches with on and off mode...
Pleasing her is plainly impossible
Is this a gift of roses or a bag of thorns?

And now the butterfly stops flying…

Can't you see he is a beast?
Must be treated as a savage
Whether I am submissive or not
If his love is really unconditional
He should give without restraint
Shouldn't judge me with his mama
Or attempt to transform me by force
When I have my own destiny to fulfill
Thinks dangling makes one a man
Snores and bores me to death
I'd rather live alone in my island
Than breathe this complex cobweb!

And now the butterfly stops flying…

Like termites after the rain

Wingless together they must find a way
Or be devoured separately…

2nd April, 2009.

HUSBANDMAN

He gives so freely sometimes
Becomes niggardly sometimes
Behaves childishly sometimes
His wisdom runs off sometimes
As wormwood, tart sometimes
As pure honey cute sometimes
He yearns for love sometimes
Fends off affection sometimes
Craves for solitude sometimes
Flows with the pack sometimes
Shouts and screams sometimes
Whispers and grunts sometimes
So weak and baffled sometimes
Bubbles with vigour sometimes
Mislays his bearing sometimes
In giant strides lead sometimes

This is why he needs a consort
Who'll stand his ups and downs
As roses and thorns grow as one
Even as day and night are apart
So he can have a sturdy household

24th October, 2004.

FEMININITY

Feelings of bitterness and control
Substitutes for that of submission
Since they cry for their liberation
From the pious prison of femininity

They flutter from the cells at home
Wandering from vales to podiums
Screaming their new found liberty
And their litter loiters in their trail

Brilliant scarlet flames of affection
Are transformed to grays of acidity
Tender silky meadows of rosy petals
Mutate to shrunken spikes of angst

Few reckon there are no prison walls
A noble and a glorious business it is
To be a heart fondly following a head
Patiently waiting on the master above

She will be called blessed at the gate…!

16th April, 2009.

BED OF ROSES

Is it the rose that batters the thorns?
Or the thorns that bruise the rose?
The flowers take the shine each day
The thorns take the shame always
Can't the rose take the shame today?
And the thorns for once the glory?

She left him to die by the dry brooks
But the ravens have not gone extinct
So, they brought him his pen and books
And serenity to stay still in the heat

Tares and wheat grow in this ground
Who knows the truth from falsehood?
Outsiders will always remain outsiders
Be it a bed of roses or thicket of thorns
For a bed of roses, one shreds the thorns
And for a hell of thorns both go to war

Yet a day must come when the tares
Have to be estranged from the wheat
For one seems not good for the other

20th May, 2009.

LAMENTATIONS

Swiftly, softly as a sparrow
Her fervour flutters away
Laden with tons of sorrow
To another heart to prey

Her heart freezes with hurt
And as wax her roots spread
Screaming in dying distress
Within the fat fiery furnace
Of her misery and loneliness

Led by the frightful fantasy
Of her brimful empty pride
She hurries out of the city
To sit in the brim of solitude
Where the lofty live to brood
Covenants wrecked in haste
Truths they will never face…

Who'll grieve her pale roses?
And who will sing her a dirge?

2nd March, 2004.

GREEN CARD

Would I ever see him again?

Two years was our agreement
Since he left on that old train
I have not seen any mansion
Springing up in our courtyard
My wardrobe remains tattered
Our kids are now out of school…

Yes, he was to stay two years
Then begin to send us dollars
To free our name from the list
Of those feeding from the bin
Now our home is at the verge
Of hitting a very sturdy storm…

The grapevine has come alive
About your romance with another
Is it for fun or for the green card?
What is her colour, white or black?
When you cuddle her in your arms
Do you feel her love or our dollars?
If it is love, then come home now!

When will I see you again my love?
Do not need the dollars any more
At nighttime when it gets so cold
Would the dollar give me warmth?
I have become sickly staying alone
Like a rose crushed by the weather
And you know I can't double deal.

Our kids are dying to see you again
Their questions are making me mad
Please you must return to us at once
The two years we agreed is now five
I do not need the dollars anymore

You must come back home to us now
If not, I will do something stupid.

27th April, 2006.

COBWEBS

Treachery becomes her second skin
At midnight she disappears to the city
Her tongue flying freely like a new fan
Tearing down every wind without pity

Shamelessly she tears down her roses
Searing every of her nerve and chord
Prized receptacle for tomorrow's seed
Just to reinforce her degenerate greed

All broadways shrink to deserted alleys
Her wrinkles become cavernous valleys
As torrents of her seclusion swell high
Yet she wards off everyone with a sigh

But her ancient spindle continues to spin
Fresh silky cobwebs for another quarry
Will she ever be crowned a queen
Sitting atop the pack of broken paths…?

May, 2009.

GOLDFISH

Carefully she stared on
Lost in the maze of time
Not to be found out…

What a hoax!

She lied the first time
Maybe a million times
Like a petite goldfish
Her shine suits a tag
Blazing in her wake
Her tongue twisting
Fraught with deceit
Uniquely flapping…

Oh what deception!

To lie about her colour
Now I am weighed down
With this tempting twinge
Out in the network of time
Now what to believe… bizarre

MOTHER-IN-LAW

But they are of two generations apart
So they speak in two different tongues

They leave but cannot cleave together
As her toy is still in her cradle's court…

Now she is torn between two minds
Between her folly and her resentment
As they have sent the old wine to hell
And the new is so sturdy to be bottled
Yet her umbilical cord clinches so fast

She would not let her new flowers bud
Nor her the nursery become a prototype
As her seed they must travel her course
And become like the old stone bramble

Now he's been put to sleep after supper
A meal of love potion with a death wish…

And she is lost like a seagull in the deep
Urged on by one dreadfully experienced…

4th June, 2009.

ADVENTURERS

Knows all the fountains in the city
Drinks from them and still is thirsty
Every mound and hill knows his steps
Samples all curves and remains empty
As his seed is lost abroad, he is barren

Who is he that wears a scent
And desires to pull down a saint?
He's like a man wearing a mask
Of dust and stands in a heavy rain…
Like a ghost learning to disappear
Appears and fails how to disappear

She stands before her large mirror
Smiling, happy he had kissed the dust
The thorns in flesh for ten decades
The thistles that smear her beauty
Made her speed snail-like…

Everyone heralded her gallantry
Got the pulpit filing for her gold
And praise from the polluted pews
Lost and in the labyrinth of perfidy
Yet she drinks on intoxicated

June, 2009.

LOST AT SEA

Does she not know their new ship
Is heading for a dreadful iceberg?
They've been in this seething sea
Inspired by a vengeful vain vanity
Screaming of friends and admirers
Counsel of those godly and prudent
Fail as rudder to steer them ashore
The tired tempest tears rearward…

As they take this adventure together
Through the thickets of the jungle
Through the depth of the severe sea
And the parched places of the desert
Will they outlive the accusers' sting?

Would they berth together ashore
Would they path in different tides
Or be ruined in the deepest blue
Without any memory of their sail?

She cannot discern her flower beds
Roses planted by her hands now frail
For brambles battle to seize her field
As butterflies no longer come around
And the amazing hummingbird extinct

Wrinkles like waves line up her face
For fury floods her hurt heavy heart
And a veil clouds the seed of offence
Will they all be saved from this night?

DEOXYRIBONUCLEIC ACID

The masquerade lost his mask to urchins
In broad- daylight in the market place…
With fresh leaves he conceals his identity
And waits for darkness to flee for safety

Dwarfs and local dogs assembled together
To discuss who pulled down the city gate
Old tales buried with dried bones laid bare
On the table the doorway to the new world

They are seven and the fourth is a stranger
A thistle growing amid a new bed of roses
A crocodile in the train of blind ducklings
And the mother duck is blaring werewolf…

He that bends to peep into another's anus
Will surely find two things, 'this' and 'that…'
A bit of something or maybe nothing
Yet without risk there is never a reward

So, if the goat in the house is black or white
Or, the sheep in the farm is black and white
Do not accompany them to the airport
Or, fables like a goat has become a stallion,
And the sheep transformed to a unicorn
And chickens now hound hyenas for dinner…

And Aesop in the walls of your courtyard
Will reincarnate and return again to school
Maybe yester night's toadstool is a canopy
Don't mind I will ride my dog to the market…

ALBATROSS

That one day the bell will toll for me
Is not the burden upon my shoulder

That my foes will cast off restraint
As soon as my demise is published
Some in their closet, others publicly
Partying my exit, does not ache me

That while some will be mourning
Others are arranging props to snatch
That my creditors might seek a fight
Or that my debtors will take a flight
Do not take away my sleep for now

Certainly, those that love me will weep
Surely, those I love won't be comforted

My pain will be those I feel would die
When my departure is made public
Those that say I smell like sweet roses
Those I thought would go mourning
That they'll go wild popping champagne
Dancing tango in uncontrolled obsession…

The unknown, the uncertain
If I could but see the morrow
Many a feast I would have
This is my shadow, my albatross

22nd February, 2009.

EMBARGO

You must obtain a visa for Jerusalem?
For she has ascended to glory ground
Whilst the pilgrims dwell in the valley
In her high hills kissing is out of bound
Feelings have become totally forbidden

It is the wind that makes her ascend
It comes from those singing her praise
They will never let her know the truth
So, they won't stir up her indignation
And lose corals flowing from her rapids

They live only to venerate the villain
Swell daily as they vilify the virtuous
Straight paths they search out to twist
Smooth trails they crave to roughen
Every rose they see they turn to a thorn

Every night he stays awake brooding
And in the morning, he pleads, hoping
Not to end as the patient dog that died
Waiting for the fattest bone far away…

HARBINGERS

Before the Lord comes
Love and hate will abide
Together like Siamese twins…

As roses and thorns
In a barren backyard
Bitterness and sweetness
Will flourish side by side
Before the master comes…

Before the master comes
Trust and deceitfulness
Will flow together
Like oil and water
Leaving smiles and scars
In the hollow hearts of many

Before the Lord comes
Peace and war will rage
Amid peoples and nations
Building and destroying
The fountain of the saints
The wicked, an added time…

Hope, an oasis of kindness
Will dry out as in a drought
Then fear, will cause many pain…

But when He comes -
The ocean of love
The prince of peace

The mirror of justice
The master of the universe -
Everything will be made new again

22nd January, 2000.

EYE-OPENER

You will never know how deep
Hatred runs, when smiles reign
If deception and pretense thrive
Your finest friend, secretly a rival
Until revealed you are only a toy
Confined, preserved for extinction
Like thorns when their roses fade…

You will never know how foggy
Hearts of those in folly you adore
With your cards open on their table
Their tedious thoughts sport wings
And as keen current they flow veiled
Unrevealed you are a blindfolded bat

You will never know the slippery path
For decades so sheepishly you shuffled
Or the spleen of the cobra you cuddled
Or the seas of treachery rising over you
Sweet venoms whirling in your bowels
Bursting, yet impotent but for destiny

You will only know when it is daybreak
As groaning breaks down bars and hurdles
And your pain and trials confirm patience
Then in glory some deep things revealed…

December, 2008.

ADMIXTURE

Countless waters cannot down love
Flying fiery flames cannot devour love
Eager quicksand cannot overcome love
Furious lightening can never strike love
Persistent tempest cannot shatter love
The scorched Sahara cannot subdue love
So, pressures of life should not stop love
For love is constant like roses and thorns
Growing together as faith and patience
Become a celestial mix and test for life…

Only when this love is true and celestial…

August, 2009.

CROWNLESS

Sometimes we crawl to grab a chicken
When naively she sits in the open field
Scraping for worm on a craggy ground
Unaware the talons of a hovering kite

For a decade they seek heaven's face
Another season groves in odd places
They are now weary of this groping
Picking live roses in patched places

Why should they visit a carpenter
When they seek lines and fishhooks?
Why should they contract covenants
With oath breakers and dream killers?

Why would they propose their future
With people in soul-ties with the past?
Why would they call on the elephant
Just to learn the swift ways of the eagle?

Shouldn't a hen feeding openly be discreet?
As passing shadows could be a hungry hawk
Seeking exposed stubborn straying chicks?
Sometimes a cheerful bird need not sing…

June, 2009.

WILD HOG

In the precinct of the sanctuary
By the sanctification of the body
The body becomes a deadly vitriol
Offered for a saint's untimely passage
He, divinely sent to sanctify, curses
He, sent to bring light, a veil of doom
He serves spikes in a cup of red roses…
    As Judas deals his seared soul for gain

A call for an embrace from the pulpit
Turns chilly current for hallowed harm
A venture to test force of a new charm
As a sister is transformed to an invalid

All in the precinct of a sacred sanctuary
A mirror of our bequest to his comeliness…

24th June, 2009.

PORTRAITISTS

They paint pictures of me
Leaving ugly brush strokes
Trying to reveal unkindness
But they can't fix the colours
That portrays my real identity…

So, when I notice my pictures
All over pages of their journals
Billboards in their soiled cities
When their tongues wag away
In dreadful unequaled chuckles
Like a rose flower without roses
Others in graveyard undertone
How repulsive my pictures are
I do not lift my fist to fight them
Or raise my blood to fight myself
Within me I only exhale bravely
Because their prints only reflect
My weakness that they can see
Their wickedness they cannot see
By their human, prejudiced eyes…

August, 2005.

AHITOPHEL

They gather to show her the plains
Borders where trees have no grains
Where roses grow without prickles
Where love blossoms without kisses
She is green in this forlorn footpath
Where three-fold-cords are wrecked

From their own collapsing cocoons
Where they live like feral baboons
They smile as old cracks on bottles
With their blood shroud falsehoods

Counselors with spleen in their pot
Honey flows freely from their tongues
Like honey flowing from fangs of vipers…

TARES & WHEAT

He sowed seeds of separation
Fabricated fallow falsehood
In testing their commitment
He sent out an angel…

Incapable of discovering the one
Fashioned flawlessly for him
Before their early morning glory
He's faded away as the sunup dews

He threw her out into waiting arms
For she is pure gold in rags
Mild balm that'll calm any nerves
If our defects dare the fire of trials
And flee not until the tares burn-off …

You plot to make me hate her
One that brings me sunshine
Should I hate a God- sent one?
That helps to steady my sanity…

Tell me should I hate the star
That brings much happiness
To a life termed to be joyless
One that discovered my blade
Was blunt and needed filing…

You keep trying to steal her
Buying her flowers and gifts
Without a smile she ignores you
You fly kites of her disloyalty

In my blue sky there is no space…
For this one I intend to preserve
For the cold nights and clear mornings
A judge or jury cannot this one condemn
For this oxygen brings life to spike my veins…

3rd February, 2008.

PARADOX

Is this what love means?
That the heart that loves is crushed
In the hungry graters of a fresh mill
The heart that does not love, applauded?

Is this what true love means?
The soul that loves becomes a fool
Banished, mislaid in a desolate island
And the soul that loves not, celebrated!

Is this what love means to you?
The one that loves is daily denied
Loving warmth, care and fondness
And the one that loves not, fattened?

Is love not truly a fool
For those who love pertinently suffer
Those that love not, above all triumph?

Is love the rocks so hard?
Good seeds live enduring in odd mates
Their hearts can't bend to see heavens…?
But linger in the depths of foolish pride

Is love not queer?
As roses fit for garlands of kings
Line up the beds and junkyard of beasts
Menacing, yet adored by blindfolded beauties…

February, 2007.

STEP BY STEP

Seems I'm frail at listening
Not because I do not care
To know the way you feel
Somehow it is my failing -
Not having patience ideal
By offering my ears totally…

I do not interpose willfully
To spite you into a recoil
What has become a weight
Is this stuffed stress of mine…

I come to you open minded
With no concealed agenda
A desire to be close to you
But I need your dedication
Then, we will get so intimate
Hopefully our love will grow
Blossoming like true roses
Shining in our conversations…

11th May, 2004.

SOLITUDE

Why can't they see the twinge
That weighs him down everyday
So openly he is called an infidel
Though he is still firmly in faith
And will offer his life for his own

Here comes the scream again…
"Take care of your duty you infidel!"

Why can't they feel the emptiness?
As he gropes to sand-fill the space
Shame of crawling while others fly
Infamy of tottering as others shine…

And the irritation continues…
"I cannot suffer this anymore
I did not dot these lines to suffer …"

He should not be alone yet he is
Lives with his spouse and offspring
He who finds a wife finds a good thing
This rose comes with so many thorns

As tales of impotency fills the city
So intense the battle for a destiny
Yet no one knows to lend a voice
To help hoist this white standard

Without a voice he is lost at home
With his honesty a Jew in the street
Yet he must carry on in this pursuit

Hopeless yet hopeful of redemption

2nd July, 2009.

IN THE WILDERNESS

There comes certain lovely storm of life
In the heat the world becomes a furnace
Everyone, even your friends fade away
And you become so hard to understand
As they imagine if you are day or night
Or wonder if they are now deaf or not…

Your words merely sounding Greek
And your spirit in this whirlwind fights
So you are not deserted as a neurotic
In the sanatorium in their naive minds -
A living dead in the borders of the dead…

Your gentle palm caresses your face
But for warmth, spiky blades prick
Your drained screaming heart
Yet no one comes around to hear you
You must carry on to the end alone…

You are not asking for handouts
But for empathy and patience, and care
Only the creator can touch men's hearts

3rd July, 2009.

HUMBLED

We smile like we know not how to cry
Though in secret weep in our closet
As happy people we should not sigh
As iced ponds we cannot flow high
As stones our pain must be cloaked …

Take a look at these gloomy faces
Like old masks dyed in new kaolin
Hearts burdened in fiendish grief
Lives mislaid in a maze of misery
Choices made without a sure lead
Was it really without a sure guide?
A sojourn with ignoble daughters
Brought in with gladness and joy
Still living in their father's house

Lack in the sea of amazing riches
Riches thriving under subjection
Faces smiling, heads prostrating
Feet dragging, arm's humbled
Crowns fallen, yet as kings reigning
Altars bleeding as priests pleading…

8th August, 2009

TIMES LIKE THIS

At times like this when you are cut off
Loved ones disappear for your shame
As you fight to line up amongst friends
They swiftly fade away leaving you lost

It's times like this that make you wonder
The way out of the desperations of life
You've prayed yet the heaven is as steel
In frightful despair your loose wings fail

At times like this you don't know whom
To confide in as whispers flutter freely
Your perceived friends become prickles
On your fumbling feet seeking light

Times like this when love like rose fades
In its place heartless thorns spring forth
And as every brook begins to desiccate
You are trapped, incapable of breathing

It's times like this that you begin to die
The hidden strength lying waste inside
Begins to flow like wine in a winepress
It's at times like this that all is revealed
I love you does not mean I'll die for you…

7th October, 2009.

THE WIND BLOWS

When the wind blows light comes upon us
and makes our life glow.

When the wind blows God's glory reveals
our today for tomorrow.

When the wind blows it brings rain
of healing upon desolate destinies

When the wind blows it reveals
man's oddity before God's faithfulness

When the wind blows the secret of
the earth's treasures are revealed

When the wind blows it spews the air
we need for the breath of life

When the wind blows the trees bow
flowers and reeds dance

When the wind blows waves in the sea
clap their hands and send sweetness to mankind

When the wind blows butterflies float
and glide in awesome glory

When the wind blows roses bloom, die
but thorns abide for more seasons

Let the wind blow around you

so you will see all that are about you.

February, 2010.

ANOTHER DAY

I see the rains as they come down
And the floods as they rise
The joy, the pain and deaths
That attend their way…

I see the sun shine
In its brightness hope, heat and strokes
And the dryness of the land, the people
Then she sets with dreams emptied…

I see the flowers in their beauty
As they bloom in our dying estates
The butterflies as they gaily glide
Birds sucking their sour nectars
And their ugliness as it fades…

I see children learning to walk
Joyful as they learn the balancing act
Oblivious these steps, their first steps
Might never run the fields they see
Fields littered with landmines…

I see mothers celebrate
The birth of their bundles of joy
Soon to wail as their seed is cut from them
By hunger and sickness
By the insanity and the toxin
From the wild roses in our high places

I see fathers lose their voice,
And their mates take off

With their best friends,
Lovely flowers now thorns fit for fire
Their sons cut from them
Their angels roam the city
Stripping and spinning for stipends
I see, we see, and we keep mute
We all do nothing…

18th May, 2008.

TOMORROW

I am a child who mistakenly breaks his mother's plate
waiting for the obvious reproof he will soon receive
When his mother returns from the market…

I am a man waiting outside the labour room
for the first cry, sign that the seed he sowed now lives…

I am a wine tapper expecting his in-laws tomorrow, but
unable to sleep today, praying that his chi fills his keg
with the palm tree's divine nectar to retain his place
as a worthy in-law in the heart of his 'kindly' guests…

I am like a rose whose flowers have been plucked out
With thorns abandoned for the sun to dry out…

I am the wind on a dry savannah plain with dust only
And parched sand left as residue for its yesterday glory;

I am like the sun, I set today; I will rise again tomorrow…

23rd December, 2010.

About The Author

Obiorah Momife is a graduate of the University of Port Harcourt, Rivers State, Nigeria. He worked as a Cabin Crew in the former Nigeria Airways for more than a decade. He has a Certificate and a diploma in Public Relations from Nigeria Institute of Public Relations (NIPR) and Business Education Examination Council (BEEC) respectively. He coordinates Men's Accountability Network (MAN), an Interactive forum for men and, Think Right Choose Right Initiative, an empowerment platform for young people. He also has interest in the area of Total Customer Care/Services. He is a well-traveled youth mentor with a passion for the restoration of sound values and principles in the family and society. He has two other unpublished collections of poems titled *"Crosses" and "So Far Away"*. He is married to Isioma, and they are blessed with four lovely children, Somtochukwu, Chimesomma, Ofiligonachukwu and Kamsisochukwu.

www.ingramcontent.com/pod-product-compliance
Lightning Source LLC
LaVergne TN
LVHW041123150826
845673LV00007B/2176

* 9 7 8 9 7 8 9 1 5 7 4 7 1 *